The Uncuddibles

A Heroes Tale

Written and illusrated by
RJ Thompson

Dedications

I wish to dedicated this series of books to my own little princess, my four year old daughter Bella. She has helped and inspired me throughout. Albeit that my career has taken me on a different path, my passion has always remained within the creative arts. Whether it be writing songs, drawing comics, graphic design or learning to play different instruments, I find the challenge of creating something from scratch within my own mind addictive.

This is my first illustration and I have no idea how this will play out, but having had my little girl with me all the way, listening and learning about the Uncuddibles, constantly asking questions and excited to see the next page, gave me the encouragement to see it through.

The opportunity to share my ideas and creativity is very daunting however clearly inspired by my own childhood heroes and memories, I look forward to bringing small Easter eggs into my own little adventures for the Uncuddibles of which hopefully everyone will enjoy as much as my daughter.

If nothing else, the fact that I have a tangible book that I created from front to back sitting on my little girls shelf means the world to me.

I hope you all enjoy the world of the Uncuddibles.

RJ Thompson

The Uncuddibles

A Heroes Tale

Written and illusrated by
RJ Thompson

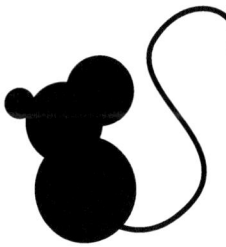

"Although we're not on every page,
Keep your eyes out, no matter what your age!"

One cloudy night in a far away land.
Stood a factory of toys forgotten by man.

A basement with puddles and holes in the walls.
Lived a small group of bears called 'The Uncuddibles'.

Their fur was tattered, in need of repairs.
Thrown out by their owners and replaced with new bears.

They huddled together and all appeared swell.
All bar one, had a sad story to tell.

First there was Bulk, a big bear with a huge heart.
Bulk was so big that he turned most rooms to dark.
Bulk always helped his friends out of danger.
But poor old Bulk also suffered with anger.

Bony the bear had a hole in his chest.
He was missing both eyes but tried nevertheless.
Clever he was, always looked out for mischief.
If it was broken, Bony knew how to fix it.

Little bear Dee always looked beautiful.
Until one day when she fell off her foot stool.
Her clean white dress, now covered in spatters.
Red, blue and yellow, but that didn't matter.

Then a lost bear engraved, with writing that said.
This bear is the property of little Clark Dent.

Shadow was the smallest and Dash moved quickly.
Creepy had crawlies and his fur was quite sticky.

Many of the others had stories to share.
About how they received their bear wear and tear.

"Cheer up bears, tonights the night!" said Clark Dent.
"That big bright star is right over our heads!"

"Easy for you to say, you were lost and not dumped. Just thinking about it gives me the hump" said Bulk.

Then all of a sudden with a whoosh and a smash.
The big bright star hit the ground with a crash!
All of the bears were excited to see.
What could it be that hit the old apple tree?

One by one they climbed over the bricks.
Shadow was worried so she picked up a stick.

A big puff of smoke and a strange funny noise.
Was it a dog? A cat? Another furry toy?
The clouds cleared away, Dee got rid of the lot.
The Uncuddibles gasped... "A little Robot!"

B3 was his name and he was clearly quite lost.
Upset that his spaceship was shattered and bust.

Bulk used his strength to collect up the parts.

Bony used his brains...

Dash and Dee
helped out Clark.

The Uncuddibles all worked together as one.
Then poor old Creepy, hurt his thumb.
He screamed and he cried, all his bugs ran away...

But then B3 fixed him up and saved the day.

The morning sun rose and all the work was done.
"Building a spaceship was such great fun!" said Dash

The Uncuddibles waved goodbye to see B3 off.
But he came out of his ship with a rather large box.

"Thank you my friends, for fixing my ship.
Amazing team work deserves a great gift.
I'm off to a galaxy far far away.
Perhaps you will come and visit one day.

Inside this box, a gift I did make.
With special jam sauce from a very special place.
Enjoy your feast and your powers within.
Use them wisely and do lots of good things." Said B3.

With a bang and a click the big doors slammed fast.
"MAY THE SAUCE BE WITH YOU!" shouted B3...then...

"Enjoy your feast and powers within.
I wonder what's inside this big shiny thing? Said Clark.

Bulk opened the box and out burst a cake.
Yum yum thought Shadow, "I wonder how it tastes?"

Slops and slurps as the Uncuddibles tucked in.
Special jam sauce ran down each furry chin.

Their full tummies rumbled with joy inside.
Then all of a sudden to Clark's surprise...

A funny feeling hit Clark with a wham!
Could it be that special jam?
Clark felt stronger, then in the blink of an eye.
Clark rose off the ground, for now he could fly!

Bony's hole in his chest had disappeared.
He now had special eyes between those furry ears.
Bony's chest glowed with a bright white light.
To help him see in the darkest of nights.

Bulk grew bigger and even stronger.
Bulk wasn't angry any longer.

Dash's gashes were fixed with a plaster.
Quick before, he was now even faster!

Dee's tatty dress was no more.
Dee jumped so high she shook the floor!

Shadow kept things nice and simple.
Shadow became so quick and nimble.

Creepy's paws now even more sticky.
This helped Creepy climb walls very quickly.

The special jam sauce had done its trick.
All the bears were clean and fixed.
With brand new powers for each one.
The Uncuddibles were ready for lots of fun.

But then...

Exhausted from their crazy day.
The Uncuddibles fell asleep amongst the hay.

While the bears were sound asleep.
The mice were sneaking round their feet.
Sniffing what there was to take.
They came across the magic cake.

They took the crumbs inside their hole.
They filled up all their little bowls.
A pop! A crack! A whizz and wham!...

Each mouse turned green!
That blooming jam!

The Uncuddibles awoke all excited and fresh.
"I can't wait to put my new powers to the test.
We'll use them wisely and for only good things.
Imagine all the joy we can bring" yawned Dee.

**With that the Uncuddibles got ready to play.
I wonder what adventures they'll have today...**

THE UNCUDDIBLES SERIES

BOOK ONE - A Heroes Tale :
The Uncuddibles origin. A group of unwanted bears strike lucky with an unexpected visitor. Rewarded for their kindness, the bears receive some special gifts.

BOOK TWO - Bony and the Ghost Dusters :
The barn is no place to go if you believe in ghosts. The Uncuddibles team up to tackle a spooky problem for the animals in the barn.

BOOK THREE - The Hay Team, a friend in need :
The Uncuddibles receive a message from above. B3 is in need of help, but how will they get to a planet so far far away. The Uncuddibles seek the help of the Hay Team to build a special spaceship. (COMING SOON)

BOOK FOUR - Ping Pong :
It's summer and the Uncuddibles are enjoying playing in the sun until it all goes wrong and their ping pong ball gets stuck at the top of the factory chimney. Who can overcome their fear of heights and climb up into the clouds. (COMING SOON)

Available to buy at Amazon.com / Amazon.co.uk
Follow The Uncuddibles on facebook and twitter :

@theuncuddibles

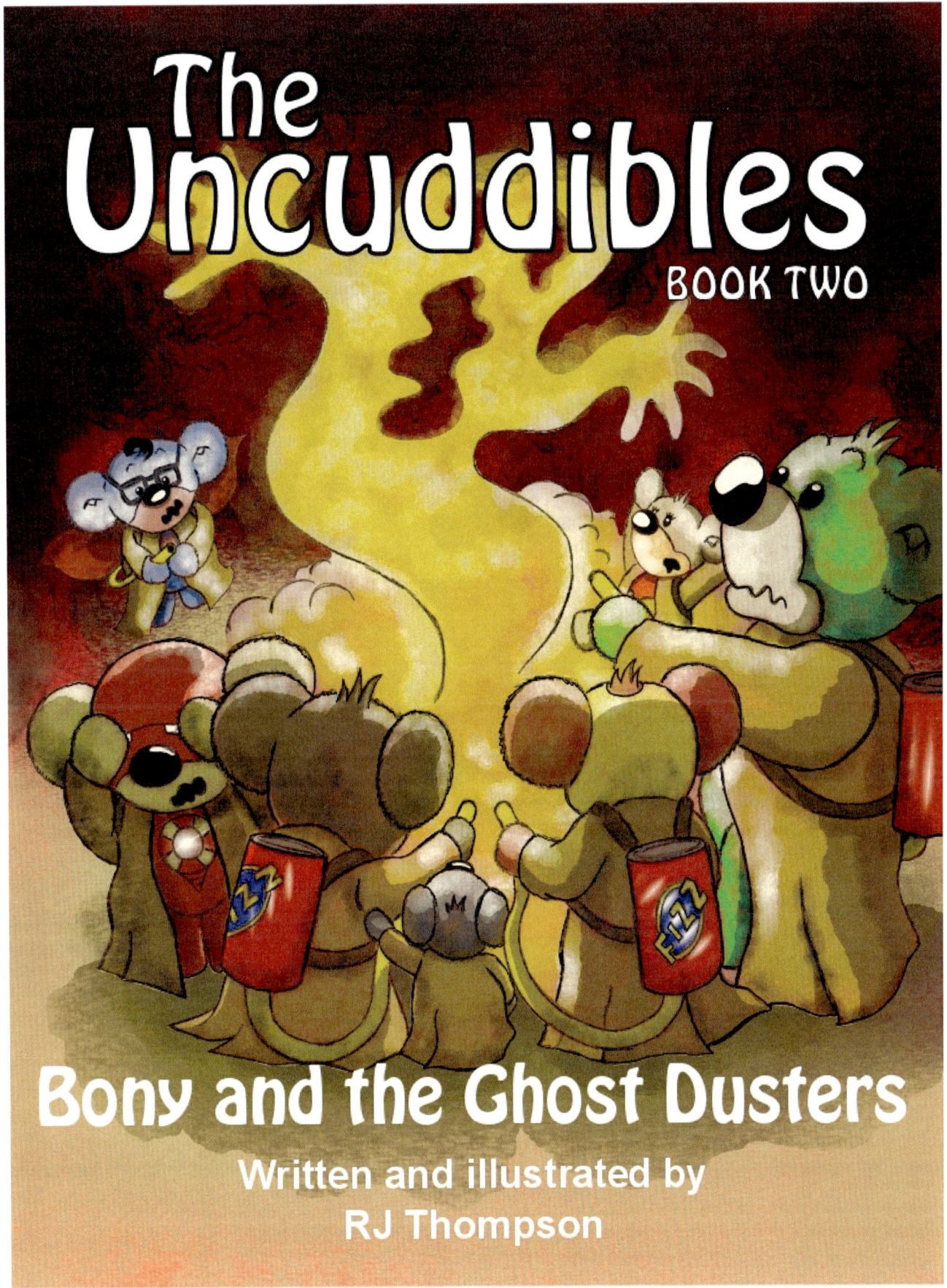

Made in the USA
Lexington, KY
24 June 2018